The Ugly Duckling

Fairy Tale Classics
STORYBOOK

One summer Mother Duck had a nest full of eggs. The nest was near a pond, where cattails grew and dragonflies flew. Mother Duck sat on her eggs to keep them warm, until the day when they would hatch. When that day came, little ducklings climbed out of their shells and ran around, filling the air with the sound, "cheep-cheep-cheep-cheep."

But there was one egg that didn't hatch with the rest.

When the last egg finally hatched, out came a duckling quite different from the others.

"There's a funny duckling," Mother Duck thought to herself while they were swimming one afternoon. "This one is white instead of yellow, and a little bigger than the rest." Even so, Mother Duck loved her special duckling.

But the others weren't so nice.

"Look at you!" said a grown-up duck one day. "You're an ugly duckling. You don't belong here with the rest."

The grown-up duck pushed away the odd duckling with its beak.

After that, things grew worse. The other ducklings liked to tease their strange brother. They would nip him with their beaks and call him names.

"You're the Ugly Duckling!" they would yell.

Of course, this made the Ugly Duckling very upset. All he wanted was to be liked.

Even the wild songbirds scattered whenever the Ugly Duckling came near.

"Look out, look out, it's the Ugly Duckling!" they yelled, flying away from him.

"I must be one ugly bird," thought the sad Ugly Duckling. "I'm so ugly I don't even have a friend."

Without any friends, the Ugly Duckling had to swim by himself.

One day, all alone, he saw a flock of larger birds flying above the water. "Look at them," he said.

"They're so beautiful—the shape of their wings, the color of their heads, the way they glide through the air." He sighed. "And I am just an Ugly Duckling."

The seasons changed from summer to fall, then came cold winter and green spring. Through them all, the Ugly Duckling was on his own, unable to find a friendly face. It was a miserable thing, being alone and feeling ugly.

One night in early spring, under the light of a full moon, the Ugly Duckling saw another flock of beautiful birds. They were flying through the sky, glowing in the moonlight, and the Ugly Duckling squawked to them: "I wish I was as beautiful as you!"

But the Ugly Duckling was in for a surprise. That spring, a remarkable change occurred in him. First, his stubby little wings had grown long and strong, and with these he had learned to fly.

The Ugly Duckling was proud. "I'm not a duckling anymore," he thought to himself. Then he wondered, "I don't *feel* ugly—and if I don't *feel* ugly then I must be fine."

Then one day he flew down toward a group of elegant swans with long, curving necks. He landed near them, thinking they might hiss at him or fly away.

Instead, the swans approached him.

As they swam closer, the Ugly Duckling felt afraid because he thought he might be attacked.

"What a lovely creature you are," they told him. The Ugly Duckling felt embarrassed. He thought they were mocking him. But when he looked down in shame, what did he see? His reflection on the water—it was the face, neck and body of a beautiful swan.

"Why yes," he said, gazing at his reflection. "I am a lovely creature. And most importantly, I *feel* like a lovely creature."